Five Kids & A Monkey™
Banish The Stinkies

Grub   Munchie   Magenta   Violet   Macaroni   Noodles

ISBN 0-9653955-2-9 / Library of Congress Catalog Card Number: 96-086336

"Clean my room? Awww, Mom! Not tonight!" Grub was <u>not</u> happy, and neither was his mother.

"Young man, your room is so messy that I can't see the floor," said his mother. "And after you get this mess straightened up, I want you to march into the shower. When you're finished, make sure you put on clean pajamas, not that old T-shirt you've been wearing since Monday!"

2

"Clean your room! Take a bath! Comb your hair! Everyone around me is a clean freak!" Grub grumbled as he tossed his dirty clothes into the hamper.

He scraped peanut butter off the lamp and wiped the muddy footprints off his desk.

He poured two glasses of sour milk down the sink and tossed three mushy, brown apple cores into the trash.

He took a shower, washed his hair and even combed most of the tangles out.

I'm too pooped to find my pillow.

After all that soaping and sudsing, cleaning and combing, Grub was exhausted. He crawled into bed and pulled the covers up to his chin. And then, he had the *strangest* dream...

Can you find Grub's pillow?

(Answer on page 30.)

He dreamed that he waved to Mr. Picadilly and Penny as they passed by, but they didn't recognize him.

Who's that grungy guy?

He went into the corner store, but Mr. Gonsalez shooed him out after he left grimy fingerprints everywhere.

OUT!

He passed the bus stop and heard a man say "What is that awful smell?"

Phew! Somebody around here has the stinkies!

He peeked in the window of Bertha's Bakery, but his face was so dirty that even _he_ was scared!

SUDSY SOAP

He dreamed that giant tubes of toothpaste and bars of soap chased him all the way home.

SPARKLE BRIGHT
FLUORIDE TOOTHPASTE

Yikes! Being stinky can be scary!

Why can't I be stinky if I want to be?

The next day in the clubhouse, Grub told everyone about his dream. Magenta told everyone about Grub's argument with their mother.

"Why should anyone else care if I'm dirty or not?" demanded Grub after Magenta finished her story. "I mean, what's the <u>reason</u> Mom always wants me to take baths and scrub my nails and change my clothes?"

No one could give him a good answer. In fact, the rest of the Kids had to admit that they had some questions of their own.

I brush my teeth. Why do I still get cavities?

Why <i>do</i> Mom and Dad shower every day? They don't <u>look</u> dirty. And how come they use deodorant?

My dad says I can share books and games, but not combs, brushes or hats.

My dad says that too. I wonder why?

I think someone just made up these rules. I bet they're not very important.

This book is all about **hygiene**. Do you know what that word means? If you're not sure, look it up in the definition list at the back of the book.

Noodles shook his head. "I'll bet there are reasons each one of them is important. I say we get busy and find out what they are."

"Oh sure, but how?" Grub asked. "My Mom's got so many rules that it would take us until midnight to research all of them!"

"Why don't we split up into groups?" asked Violet quietly. "We'll gather information more quickly."

"Good idea," said Magenta. "Noodles, grab your thinking cap and come with me. We'll find out about the stinkies."

"The *stinkies*? What in the world are those?" asked Noodles.

"That's what Mom calls it when Grub and I are sweaty and dirty," answered Magenta. "Let's find out just what makes a body get the stinkies."

Come on, Noodles! I have a plan!

Oh, great! Magenta always has a plan!

6

Hmmmm, I know another place that gets kind of stinky...

Violet turned from the window and looked at Munchie and Grub. "I think the three of us should investigate someplace totally different."

"Like where?" asked Munchie.

"Never mind. Just put your thinking caps on. Are you ready?"

READY!

Oh, if I have to!

"FOLLOW ME!" called Violet, and they started spinning 'round and 'round, getting smaller and smaller until **SPLAT!**

They landed on something hard and shiny and wet.

OOF!

What is this weird place?

WOW! This will be fun!

Before you turn the page, can you guess where the kids have landed?

Unscramble these letters to find the names of the teeth Mr. Picadilly is using to bite his sandwich.

CIRSOSNI, OLSMAR, USCIPSD

(Answers on page 30.)

WATCH OUT! Tuna sandwich coming in!

Grub, Violet and Munchie squeezed themselves between two teeth just as Mr. Picadilly's jaw began moving up and down and side to side. Bits of tuna and bread were getting mushed and mashed all over the place! And as soon as Mr. Picadilly swallowed, he took another bite and began the whole mess again! Needless to say, Mr. Picadilly's mouth was <u>not</u> a pleasant place to be just then!

Fun? Who said this would be fun?

Mr. Picadilly washed the last bite of sandwich down with a mouthful of milk.

Phew! Now it sure is stinky in here!

Hey, look at this!

Violet was examining a molar closely. "Most of the food has washed away, but there are still bits of bread sticking to his teeth."

Grub and Munchie pulled out their magnifying glasses just in time to watch those bits of food mix with the bacteria in Mr. Picadilly's mouth. As they watched, the food and bacteria turned into...

Ugly little Acid Men were popping up on Mr. Picadilly's teeth and even in between them! They were gnawing and clawing at those teeth as if they were trying to eat them.

Violet was puzzled. "Holes? But whatever for?"

"Because that's our job," Acid Man answered. "When you snack, we attack! Hey! Look at the time! We've only got 15 minutes left." And the Acid Men gnawed and clawed even harder than before.

Bacteria, Plaque and Acid Man!

"The bacteria in your mouth feed on the food you eat and make plaque. Plaque is the fuzzy coating you feel when teeth need brushing. As the bacteria break down the food, they form an acid –that's me, Acid Man! I make holes in the hard, shiny enamel that covers each tooth, and I'm especially strong for thirty minutes after you eat. When you eat foods that stick to teeth, like bread or potato chips, I get extra time to make holes in your tooth enamel. Now, don't tell anyone, but the only thing I'm really afraid of is a toothbrush and toothpaste, because they'll just scrub me away."

Crack the code, below, to discover Acid Man's message. Write your solution on a separate piece of paper. (Answers on page 30.)

Clue: A=1, B=2, C=3, etc.

20 8 5   8 15 12 5 19   9

13 1 11 5   1 18 5   3 1 12 12 5 4

3 1 22 9 20 9 5 19.

You have exactly thirty minutes to crack this secret code!

Everyone knows that good detectives write down everything they notice. After all, they never know what clues will be important later on. Munchie, Grub and Violet took out their notebooks and walked around Mr. Picadilly's mouth.

Grub noted that the Acid Men stopped gnawing and clawing after 30 minutes.

Munchie noted that bits of crackers and pieces of Fruiti Tooti cereal were stuck to Mr. Picadilly's back teeth. "I'll bet foods that stick to teeth are real cavity makers," Munchie thought.

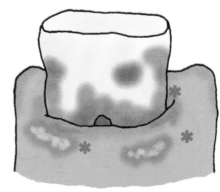

Violet noted that some teeth were stained. The gums had pulled way back and there were big, ugly sores on the sides of the mouth. "We've got to get to the bottom of this," Violet thought.

But Violet didn't have time to get to the bottom of anything, because Mr. Picadilly's mouth suddenly opened wide. In came a big toothbrush loaded with green fluoride toothpaste.

Watch out!

Brush bristles and toothpaste foam started flying all over the place! Mr. Picadilly brushed the front, back and top of each tooth. Finally, he took a big drink of water and swished it around and around.

Grub was dripping wet and had toothpaste stuck to the end of his nose. "This is the worst case we've ever had!"

Violet interrupted him. "Did anyone notice how much better it smells in here?" The boys took a deep breath.

"Look! Most of those creepy Acid Men have been brushed away," said Grub.

Except for a couple stuck in between his teeth.

"Maybe that's why my Mom is always telling me to floss, floss, floss," said Grub. "Flossing gets rid of the food between teeth."

I just don't get it.

Munchie was confused. "I brush with a fluoride toothpaste to get rid of food and Acid Men. So how come I still get cavities?"

Violet looked suspiciously at Munchie's soda and his bag of potato chips.

"You know, Munchie," she said, "maybe that's because you eat all the time. Every time you eat, acid attacks your teeth for thirty minutes. And each time you sip a soda your teeth get a sugar bath, too."

The Kids ran for cover as Mr. Picadilly crammed a big wad of black leafy stuff over to one side of his mouth.

"Ugh! I've seen ball players use that — it's chewing tobacco!" cried Grub.

"Well, that explains Mr. Picadilly's sore gums and stained teeth," said Violet.

Grub started spinning 'round and 'round until ...CLUNK! He landed right back where he started from.

This is a fine time for a malfunction.

Where are you going, Grub? You haven't proved that you've learned a thing!

Me? Well, gee, I've learned <u>lots</u> of things!

"I've learned that... uh... brushing my teeth gets rid of plaque and acid," said Grub.

"And he knows foods that stick to teeth are the worst," said Munchie helpfully.

"And that chewing tobacco causes sores and rotten gums," added Violet.

"O.K., O.K.," said Acid Man. "If you can finish this rhyme, you may go. If not, you stay here and take a tobacco juice bath!"

Take out a piece of paper and help Grub fill in the missing words. If you don't, he may be stuck in Mr. Picadilly's mouth forever!

T ✗ ✗ ✗ ✗ help you talk.
They help you to **e** ✗ ✗ ,
But you must do your part
To help them stay neat.

B ✗ ✗ ✗ ✗ three times a day
to make sure they're clean.
Then use dental floss
to get in **b** ✗ ✗ ✗ ✗ ✗ ✗ .

Watch out for sticky foods
like raisins and **c** ✗ ✗ ✗ ✗ .
They're not good for teeth,
Tho' for **c** ✗ ✗ ✗ ✗ ✗ ✗ ✗
they're dandy!

But the worse thing to do,
From your mouth's point of view,
Is to use any kind of **t** ✗ ✗ ✗ ✗ ✗ ✗ ,
Especially the kind that's chewed.

(Answers on page 30.)

Choose from these words:

captives

cavities

tobacco

tenth

tooth

teeth

eek

eat

ear

blush

brush

brash

between

betwixt

crash

candy

crabby

While Grub was desperately trying to solve Acid Man's riddle, Magenta and Noodles were having quite an adventure of their own. As they left the clubhouse, Magenta decided to hop onto the skin of the first person she saw...and Penny Picadilly just happened to be walking by with her dog at that very minute.

A second later, they were spinning 'round and 'round until they landed SPLAT! on the back of Penny's neck.

"It's like a jungle here!" said Noodles.

"Don't worry, that's just hair," said Magenta. "But what is Macaroni doing?"

Let's go get her!

O.K!

Macaroni was playing with odd looking things that reminded Noodles of giant cornflakes. He examined one through his magnifying glass.

"It's a dead skin cell," he reported. "Skin cells live only a month before they get replaced with new ones. I guess they just flake off when they die."

"That's one good reason to wash," said Magenta. "Who wants to be covered in a bunch of old dead skin cells?"

CLICK!

Grub will never believe this!

Over 14 MILLION dead skin cells flake off your skin every single day!

Just then, Penny's dog spotted a cat. With a loud bark, the dog took off. Penny had to run as fast as she could to keep up.

BARK BARK BARK BARK BARK

"Got an umbrella? It's starting to rain!" shouted Noodles.

"That can't be rain," said Magenta.

"It's not coming <u>down</u> on our heads, it's coming <u>up</u> from Penny's skin. And it's salty, too."

What is the "salty water" coming from Penny's skin? Answer on page 30.

The Kids dried off. Next, they slid down a strand of Penny's hair. They noticed how oily it was.

CLICK!

They hiked down an arm and noticed that bits of dust and dirt were stuck to Penny's skin.

This skin feels sticky.

Look at all the dirt stuck in this sweat.

They noticed there were teeny tiny bacteria all over Penny's skin.

CLICK!

What is that smell??

Bacteria are mixing with the sweat. That makes the smell.

They noticed that there were two big eyes staring right at them!

Penny didn't seem the least bit happy to find two tiny people and a monkey on her arm.

"Oh, hi there!" Magenta began. "We were just, uh, looking for Macaroni! He was lost, and..."

"Never mind, I know you and your crazy detective club. You're out looking for clues to something, aren't you?" Penny demanded. "Well, what is it?"

"Gee, now that you mention it, we're gathering information for Grub," Noodles said. "We want him to understand why it's important to wash regularly."

"Well, Grub sure needs a lesson in keeping clean," said Penny. "He's the messiest looking kid I ever saw!"

"You know, Penny, it would be really helpful if you washed your hands," said Magenta. "That way, we could see how washing changes things around here."

"I could do that," said Penny slowly. "If you two and your monkey promise to get off my arm – and never come back!"

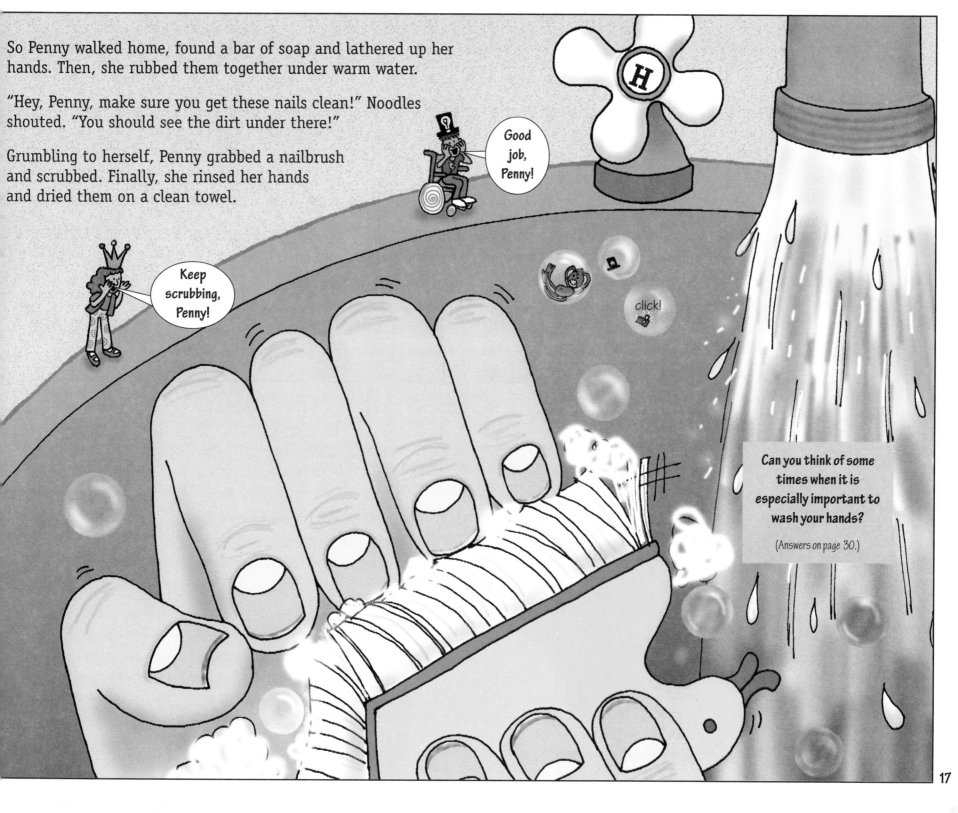

So Penny walked home, found a bar of soap and lathered up her hands. Then, she rubbed them together under warm water.

"Hey, Penny, make sure you get these nails clean!" Noodles shouted. "You should see the dirt under there!"

Grumbling to herself, Penny grabbed a nailbrush and scrubbed. Finally, she rinsed her hands and dried them on a clean towel.

Can you think of some times when it is especially important to wash your hands?

(Answers on page 30.)

Get out your mirrors, kids! You'll need them to decipher this important message.

Everyone's skin makes oil. Oil keeps skin soft and stops it from drying out. But, oil can build up and trap dirt and bacteria. When that happens — you've got the stinkies!

That's why it's important to use soap when you wash. Soap breaks down oil so water can wash it away. Try this: rub some vegetable oil on the back of your hand. Then, rinse your hand with warm water. What happens to the water drops? Now, wash the oily spot with soap and warm water. Can you see the difference?

Noodles noticed that there was less dirt and fewer dead skin cells on Penny's hands after they were washed. "Lucky thing she got rid of that bacteria, too," Noodles thought.

Give Bacteria The Boot

Noodles is right. It is good to get rid of the bacteria on your skin. To find out why, see if you can read the sentence in the block of letters, below. Use your finger to follow the letters around and around. The first letter is highlighted for you.

I	A	C	A	N	M
R	A	N	C	A	A
E	C	D	O	U	K
T	D	O	R	S	E
C	N	Y	*	E	Y
A	A	D	O	B	O
B	K	C	I	S	U

What Do You Think?

Should you wash your hands before you eat, even if they look clean? Why or why not?

(Answer on page 30.)

Magenta took out her tape recorder.

"What are you doing?" Noodles asked.

"I'm recording a memo for Grub," Magenta answered. "Memo to Grub: Washing with soap is important because it gets rid of dead skin cells, sweat, bacteria and extra oil."

Magenta and Noodles began walking up to Penny's head, when out of nowhere came a terrifying screech!

"It's Macaroni!" cried Noodles. "He must be in trouble!"

Magenta and Noodles raced toward the sound and found themselves in a thick tangle of hair. Pushing through it, they saw Macaroni surrounded by giant bugs with six arms, pointy antennae and tiny heads.

"What kind of lousy bugs are those?" Noodles shouted.

Magenta pulled out her trusty Pocket Guide to Bizarre Bugs and started flipping pages. "They're lousy all right!" Magenta cried. "They're head lice. And lice suck on blood! We've got to get out of here!"

Head Lice

Head lice are little bugs that are passed from one person to another when they share hats, hairbrushes or pillows. The lice live on the hair and scalp and suck blood through the scalp.

People don't get lice because they're dirty or because they don't wash their hair. Anyone can get lice, because they spread fairly easily.

The only way to get rid of lice is to use a special shampoo and a comb with teeth that are very close together. The comb helps to scrape the eggs of the lice, called "nits," off the hair.

Little hooks help the louse hang onto strands of hair.

nit
hair
nit
scalp

Lice irritate the scalp and make it itch.

The singular of the word "lice" is "louse."

Meanwhile, back in the clubhouse, Violet, Munchie and Grub were rinsing tobacco juice and toothpaste out of their clothes. Grub admitted that brushing his teeth three times a day might not be a bad idea.

"I'd do anything to get rid of those creepy acid guys," he said.

Munchie was just getting ready to open a bag of popcorn when a loud whirling noise filled the room. The three looked up in time to see Magenta land on the floor head first, followed closely by Macaroni and Noodles.

"What is Macaroni screeching about?" asked Grub.

"Oh, I guess something's bugging him..." said Noodles with a smile.

"We have some wild pictures to show you, Grub," said Magenta. They looked at the pictures of the dead skin cells, bacteria and dirt. Macaroni acted out his run-in with the head lice.

"Now I understand why Mom and Dad shower every day," said Magenta.

"And I know why Dad always tells me not to borrow anyone's hat or brush," said Violet.

"But what about Mom's other rules, like changing my underwear and socks every day? She never even lets me wear the same shirt two days in a row! Now, don't you think she's a little clean crazy?"

I may be able to answer that question, Grub, but first I need to look at your dirty laundry.

Excuse me?

Grub was puzzled, but he knew Violet must be on to something. He led the kids to his house and showed Violet the pile of laundry.

"Ah ha! Just as I suspected!" said Violet. "Look at all the oil and grime that comes off on the shirts!"

"So what does that prove?" asked Grub.

"It proves that it's important to put on clean clothes after your bath," said Violet. "Sweat, dirt and dead skin get on your clothes, and you don't want to put those stinkies back on a clean body."

Munchie picked up the laundry detergent and began to read the box.

Hmmm... it says 'removes dirt and stains'.

This means washing with detergent gets clothes cleaner than washing with plain water!

Which is Cleaner?

Do you think washing clothes with detergent will get them cleaner than washing with water alone?

Find two old T-shirts and make them equally dirty. Wash one in plain water and scrub it twenty times. Wash the other shirt in water and detergent and scrub it twenty times as well. Rinse both shirts in clean water, wring them out and let them dry. Which is cleaner?

Important Notice!

When you do an experiment that compares two things, it's very important to treat both things equally. Otherwise, your conclusions (results) might be wrong. In this activity, both shirts must be equally dirty. That means you must use the same kind and same amount of dirt on each. Scrub each shirt the same number of times, too. You're testing to determine if it's the soap, and not your scrubbing, that made one shirt cleaner.

"You know, it *feels* good to have clean hair and skin, and to put on fresh clothes every morning," said Magenta.

A clean body and clean clothes shows other people what you think of yourself.

Violet suddenly noticed that Grub's face was all bunched up and he looked like he had just eaten a lemon.

"Grub! What's wrong?" cried Violet.

"Uh, nothing, I'm just thinking really hard. I think...I think there's more to getting rid of the stinkies than just washing and wearing clean clothes."

"What do you mean?" asked Noodles.

"I mean that you can't just keep your *outsides* clean. You've got to keep your *insides* clean, too." said Grub slowly. "Take Mr. Picadilly. He looks neat and wears fancy clothes, but his teeth are stained because of the tobacco he chews. He's not doing a very good job of keeping his insides clean and healthy."

Then Munchie piped up.

What's That Smell?

Grub's mom told him that he's absolutely, positively not allowed to have food in his room anymore. Here's an activity to help you figure out why she made that rule.

Pour milk into two small glasses. Put one glass on the kitchen counter. Put the other in the refrigerator. After 24 hours, give them both a sniff. What do you notice? After 48 hours, sniff them again. What do you notice now?

* What would happen if you left a glass of milk in your room for a week?
* What if the old, sour milk spilled on the rug?
* What critters might visit if you left cookie crumbs and salami sandwiches around?

"I'll bet people who are really clean wouldn't spit or litter or leave soda cans all over the park, either."

Violet nodded. "That's right. People who do that make it harder for others to be clean."

That's a good point. You know, Grub, I was thinking...Grub? Where's Grub?

25

But Grub was nowhere to be found. He wasn't in the backyard or the basement or the kitchen. The Kids were just about to look in the clubhouse when Macaroni jumped up and began waving his little arms wildly. He was swatting at something that floated by.

"It's a bubble!" said Noodles. "And look, there's another!"

"Let's follow them," called Munchie.

Can you identify the different "keep clean" tools on these two pages?

(Answers on page 30.)

Grub's Rules For Keeping Clean & Healthy

1. Wipe your feet or take off your shoes before walking in the house.

2. Rinse out the sink after you brush your teeth.

3. Wash hands with soap after using the bathroom and before eating.

4. Floss once a day.

5. Replace toothbrush every four months.

6. Replace toothbrush after you've been sick.

7. Change your underwear and socks every day.

8. Never keep moldy, old hotdogs under your bed.

Can you tell why each of Grub's rules is important? Think of some clean and healthy rules that would be good for your family.

Other Stinky Stuff

Got The Itchies?

Sometimes, soap can make your skin feel tight and itchy. That's because the soap has removed too much oil and made skin dry. Switch to soap with moisturizers in it, or use lotion after your bath.

Mirror, Mirror On The Wall...

Pick up a magazine and count the ads you see for toothpaste and shampoo, soap and makeup. Some of that stuff helps you keep clean, but not all of it. Put your thinking cap on and see if you can tell which is which. Check the answers on page 30 to find out if you're right.

Finding The Stinkies

Have you seen one of these ✱ ? It's a "stinky", and there are lots of them throughout this book. Go back and find all the places where stinkies are lurking.

When You've Got A Cut

A cut means you've got an opening in your skin. That's good news for germs (they love to get inside the cut and cause a sore, red infection), but it's <u>not</u> good news for you. So what can you do about it?

Use soap and water to wash away dirt and germs. An antibacterial cream or spray will knock them out, too. Cover big cuts with a bandage until a scab has formed. And speaking of scabs, never pick one off — it's there to protect the area until new skin has a chance to form underneath.

There's a stinky now! I guess I better wash my hands!

soap & warm water

clean towel

My skin takes good care of me, and I take good care of my skin!

clean bandage

Answers

Page 7: ...... Oh, there's Grub's pillow!

Page 8: ...... incisors, molars and cuspids

Page 10: ..... Acid Man wrote his message in a special code called a <u>cipher</u>. Each letter is replaced by either another letter, number or symbol. The message? "The holes I make are called cavities."

Page 13: ..... **<u>Teeth</u>** help you talk.
They help you to **<u>eat</u>**,
But you must do your part
To help them stay neat.

<u>Brush</u> three times a day
to make sure they're clean.
Then use dental floss
to get in **<u>between</u>**.

Watch out for sticky foods
like raisins and **<u>candy</u>**.
They're not good for teeth,
Tho' for **<u>cavities</u>**
they're dandy!

But the worse thing to do,
From your mouth's point of view,
Is to use any kind of **<u>tobacco</u>**,
Especially the kind that's chewed.

Page 15: ..... The salty water is called sweat or <u>perspiration</u>. Sweating is your skin's way of keeping you cool. How? As air passes over the sweat it <u>evaporates</u> *(dries and goes into the air)*. Try this: Wet one hand. Now, blow on both hands. The one that's wet will feel cooler as air passes over it, just as your skin feels cooler when it's sweaty.

Page 17: ..... It is especially important to wash your hands after playing outside or with friends, playing with pets and using the bathroom. It's also important to wash hands after a day at school or a trip to a store.

Page 19: ..... Yes, you should wash your hands before you eat even if they look clean. Remember, bacteria are <u>microscopic</u> – that means you can't see them without a microscope. Germs just love to catch a ride on dirty fingers right into your mouth!

Page 19: ..... The block of letters reads "Bacteria can make you sick and cause body odor."

Page 26: ..... The keep-clean tools pictured on this page are a toothbrush, dental floss, soap, nailbrush, comb, brush, shampoo, box of laundry detergent, box of tissues.

Page 29: ..... <u>Shampoo</u>, <u>soap</u>, <u>laundry detergent</u> and <u>toothpaste</u> keep you clean. <u>Nail polish</u>, <u>perfume</u> and <u>mouthwash</u> may make you look cute and smell nice, but are not important for keeping you clean. However, a <u>mouth rinse with fluoride</u> is important for keeping teeth strong and healthy. <u>Sunscreen</u> protects your skin from the sun, but it doesn't keep you clean. <u>Deodorant</u> prevents odor if you sweat, but you must use it on skin that is already clean.

How come a rooster's feathers are always so neat?

Because he carries his comb wherever he goes!

What does a monster eat after it's had all its teeth pulled out?

The dentist!

Oh that Grub! He's lost a button off his shirt. Look for the button on each page of the story where you see Grub.

Dynamic Definitions

acid .... the mixture of bacteria and sugar from the food you eat; acid can eat through the enamel covering your teeth and cause cavities. Brushing and flossing remove acid.

bacteria .... teeny, tiny organisms that are sometimes called germs. The bacteria in your mouth mix with sugar from your food and cause acid.

banish .... to get rid of

cuspids .... the pointy teeth on either side of your incisors

deodorant .... a substance used to prevent or hide odor

detergent .... a cleaning agent that is often used for clothes

floss .... a special string made to clean food and plaque from between teeth.

fluoride .... a mineral added to toothpaste, some mouth rinses and even to drinking water. It helps prevent cavities by making teeth stronger.

hombre .... (pronounced AWM-bray) — a Spanish word that means "man". A "tough hombre" is someone you don't want to mess with! Who's the tough hombre in this book?

hygiene .... the practice of keeping clean and preventing illness

incisors .... the flat teeth in the front of your mouth

lice .... tiny bugs that live on the scalp and hair shaft. They are often passed around when people share hats, pillows or brushes.

malfunction .... a breakdown

molar .... the flat-topped, bumpy teeth in the back of your mouth. Molars are used to crush and grind your food.

plaque .... Plaque is a combination of food particles and bacteria which can make your teeth feel "fuzzy".That's your cue that it's time to brush!

stinkies .... the result of bacteria mixing with sweat, dirt and oil on your skin. The stinkies also happen if you leave sour milk or moldy hotdogs in your room.

sweat .... sweat, or perspiration, is made by special, teeny, tiny organs called "sweat glands" that are deep within your skin. Sweat is mostly water, with tiny amounts of salt and some other substances.

How do you stop a skunk from smelling?

Hold its nose!

Why does Silly Willy refuse to use toothpaste?

He says none of his teeth are loose!

About The Creative Attic, Inc.

Author Nina Riccio is a certified health education specialist who has been writing health education materials in collaboration with illustrator Beth L. Blair since 1986. Their most recent venture was a health and substance abuse prevention curriculum for students in grades K-6 which is currently being used in hundreds of school systems across the US.

The **Five Kids & A Monkey**™ series was born out of their desire to create lively, child-friendly books to complement the lessons being taught in school. They hope you will enjoy the series as much as they enjoyed putting it together.

Don't miss any of the great titles in **Five Kids & A Monkey**™ Series One!

❏ **Five Kids & A Monkey**™
Investigate A Vicious Virus
   (a learning adventure about germs and the immune system)

❏ **Five Kids & A Monkey**™
Solve The Great Cupcake Caper
   (a learning adventure about healthful eating and exercise)

❏ **Five Kids & A Monkey**™
Banish the Stinkies
   (a learning adventure about keeping clean and healthy)

Watch for **Five Kids & A Monkey**™ Series Two, in which the Kids explore ways to handle conflict, deal with mixed-up emotions and make the best decisions when they're faced with lots of choices.

Customer Service: If you have any questions, problems, or suggestions, please call our Customer Service Dept. at (203) 576-6716 or 888-5MONKEY (566-6539).

Also available for each book in the series: A Unit Study guide full of experiments and suggestions for further activities in other areas, plus five reproducible workpages, all for $5.00. Contact us for purchasing information.

The Creative Attic, Inc.

P.O. Box 187, Canterbury, NH 03224
voice .... (603) 783-9103
FAX .... (603) 783-0118
toll free ... 1-888-5MONKEY (566-6539)

Attention Schools, Businesses and Non-Profit Organizations:

Five Kids & A Monkey™ books and Unit Studies with reproducible worksheets are available at bulk purchase discounts for educational use. For information, call our Customer Service Department at (203) 576-6716.